ISBN 1 85854 548 X

Published by Brimax Books Ltd, Newmarket, England, CB8 7AU, 1997.
Printed in France.

Teddy and the GHOST

By Sue Inman

Illustrated by Roy Trower

Brimax · Newmarket · England

Teddy and the Ghost

Mother Bear had gone shopping. Father Bear had spent all morning changing the sheets on the beds. Teddy was bored.
"I know," said Teddy. "I'll make some mud castles in the garden."
Teddy made four mud castles. Then he built a wall joining them all together.
He dug a moat with a drawbridge and then he poured water into it. Teddy collected lots of pebbles and stuck them to the castle walls.

Teddy found four twigs and stuck them into pieces of tissue paper. Then he stuck a twig into each castle. The wind began to blow. It caught the tissue paper flags and made them flutter. Teddy was very pleased with himself. Then just as Teddy turned to go inside, he saw it. A ghost! It was big and white and drifting across the grass towards him. Teddy could see two dark patches that looked like eyes! Teddy was scared.
"AAAGH!" cried Teddy as he ran into the house. "Dad! Dad!" he yelled.

Teddy ran from room to room looking for Father Bear. He was nowhere to be found. Teddy ran back into the kitchen. Through the window he saw something strange. Father Bear was running around the garden at top speed. Teddy forgot how frightened he was and peeped around the kitchen door. Father Bear was chasing the ghost! All around the garden he ran, trying to catch it. But every time he came close to it, the ghost drifted off. Teddy thought Father Bear was very brave.

Just then Father Bear saw Teddy.
"Help me, Teddy!" he yelled. "The wind is blowing the sheets away and they're getting muddy!"
Teddy felt silly. The ghost was really a sheet! He helped Father Bear catch the sheet. He didn't tell him what he had thought it was. That evening when Teddy went to bed he was still giggling. But in the night he was woken by a strange sound.
"Wooooo!" it went. "Wooooo!"
"It's only the wind," said Teddy to himself. But he was never really sure...

Teddy Falls in Love

A new family of bears had moved next door to Teddy. Mirabelle Bear was the same age as Teddy and it wasn't long before they met. Teddy liked Mirabelle straight away. She was kind and gentle. Soon Teddy found himself thinking about her rather a lot.

"I think I must love Mirabelle," said Teddy to Mother Bear one day. "And if I love her, I should marry her."

"You're too young to get married," said Mother Bear to Teddy.
"Well, I'll wait until I'm old enough," said Teddy. "But I'll send her a Valentine's Day card and ask her to wait, too."
"That's a good idea," said Mother Bear. "Valentine's Day is next week. Maybe Mirabelle will send you a card, too."
Teddy began making his card.
He wanted it to be the most beautiful card in the world. He drew hearts and flowers and painted them brightly. When the card was finished Teddy wrote a message inside. It said: "Dear Mirabelle, I would like to marry you when I'm old enough so please wait. Love from T".

On Valentine's Day, Teddy got up early to deliver the card to Mirabelle. He didn't have time for breakfast so he took an orange to eat on the way. As Teddy walked along, who should he see but Mirabelle! He tried to hide the card behind his back, but it was too big. When Mirabelle saw Teddy she smiled. Teddy tried to grin back, but as he did, the juice from his orange squirted out of his mouth and dribbled down his chin! Mirabelle thought this was very funny, but Teddy felt silly. He turned around and ran all the way home.

Teddy was so upset he hid in his bedroom. He would have stayed there all day but Father Bear called him downstairs. A card had been delivered. It was addressed to Teddy. He opened the card. A huge smile spread across his face. On the front of the card were beautifully painted hearts and flowers, and the words inside said:
"Dear Teddy, I would like to marry you when I'm old enough so please wait, Love M".

Can you find five differences between these two pictures?